Rocco th
AND THE CASE OF MISTAKEN IDENTITY

Written by Rachel Smith and Charlie Ford

Illustrated by Jennifer Haslam

Also available to buy from **www.roccotherockstar.com**:

Rocco the Rock Star

Rocco the Rock Star and the Flower of Sascut

and

Rocco the Rock Star Swallows the Moon

First published in the UK in 2021 by Smith and Ford, UK.

Text © Rachel Smith and Charlie Ford 2021. All rights reserved.

Design © Rachel Hathaway 2021. All rights reserved.

ISBN: 978-1-9163488-4-4

Rachel Smith and Charlie Ford have asserted their right under the Copyright, Designs and Patents Act 1988 to be identified as the author of this work.

This is a work of fiction. Names, characters, businesses, places, events and incidents are either the products of the author's imagination or are used in a fictitious manner. Any resemblance to actual persons, living or dead, or actual events is purely coincidental.

All rights reserved. No part of this publication may be reproduced, stored in a retrieval system or transmitted in any form or by any means, without the prior permission in writing of the publisher, nor to be otherwise circulated in any form of binding or cover other than that in which it is published without a similar condition, including this condition, being imposed on the subsequent purchaser.

Enquiries relating to reproduction should be sent to the authors at *info@roccotherockstar.com*

www.roccotherockstar.com

Contents

Chapter 1
The break-in   4

Chapter 2
Elsie's shocking discovery   8

Chapter 3
Jasper asks for help   12

Chapter 4
The boys go on patrol   17

Chapter 5
Goodbye, old friend   24

Chapter 6
A chance encounter   29

Chapter 7
Jack makes amends   34

Chapter 8
The doggy charity day   37

Chapter 1
The break-in

Rocco and Flo loved living next door to their Mummy's friend Charlie and their doggy pals Sassie, Jasper and Magic. Unfortunately, the tunnel between their houses had been blocked up, but they'd managed to dig a hole under the fence so they could pop into each other's gardens to see each other whenever they wanted.

One particularly glorious day they were all in the garden of Mummy's house – except for one-eyed Jasper, who was having a little nap next door on Charlie's bed.

All of a sudden, Jasper thought he heard the sound of breaking glass. He listened intently for a few minutes but he was so nice and snuggly and warm he couldn't be

bothered to get up and explore. It was probably just Rocco, he thought, he was always coming over and helping himself to the doggy biscuit tin. He'd probably knocked something over – typical Rocco, jumping around all the time.

Jasper wasn't going to let Rocco get him into trouble again, so he put his head back down and within minutes he drifted off back to sleep.

A few hours later he heard a lot of commotion downstairs and then he heard Charlie cry out, "Oh no, what's happened here!"

Jasper jumped off the bed and went down to see what all the fuss was about.

"I can't believe it," Charlie said to the gang, who had now assembled in Charlie's lounge, "we've been broken into."

Rocco and Sassie looked at Jasper, who bowed his head. Flo wasn't one to judge, but even she was surprised that Jasper hadn't at least barked and Magic, well, Magic was just so chilled he went back out in the garden to lie under a tree while all the fuss died down.

"They've taken my laptop," Charlie said, close to tears. "It had all my work contacts on there, my accounts and lots of photos." Rocco glared at Jasper – how could he not have tried to stop them? He hated seeing Charlie so upset.

Jasper felt ashamed and ran up the stairs to hide under the bed. He wished he could hear and see as well as the rest of the gang. These days it seemed like he never got anything right. He put his head between his paws and felt very sad and sorry for himself.

Downstairs Sassie nudged Rocco. He got the message and got up to leave. "Come on Flo," Rocco said, "we need to go home now and leave Sassie to comfort Charlie."

As Rocco and Flo headed out of the back door, Rocco glanced back and saw Sassie gently jump up on Charlie's lap and lick her face. A pang of jealousy shot through him, but then he felt bad as he really loved Charlie. He decided there and then he would catch whoever did this and get her laptop back.

Chapter 2
Elsie's shocking discovery

Talk of the break-in was the hot topic for several days. The gang sat around and listened as Charlie told Mummy how she remembered having seen a man hanging around outside her house a couple of days before the break-in.

Once Charlie and Mummy had gone to work, Sassie gathered the others for a meeting.

"Right gang!" said Sassie. "We need to keep a look out for the man that stole Charlie's laptop. From what Charlie was saying we are looking for a man wearing a green t-shirt and shorts riding a bike with a basket on the front of it."

"Let's keep our eyes open," she continued. "Well, Jasper, keep your one eye open. If any of us see the man and we are not together we must all bark our best alert bark and make sure we do not let the man out of our sights until we are all together. Charlie will be so proud of us and we will get her laptop back."

Jasper thought to himself, I may only have one eye but I'm going to show the gang and Charlie that I can get it right. I will find the thief that broke into our house and stole Charlie's laptop.

A couple of days later whilst walking on the High Street, Sassie overheard Elsie, an elderly lady who lived behind Charlie's house in the retirement flats, telling a lady who was helping her across the road that her shopping trolley had been stolen. Elsie said that she had left her trolley outside the pet shop for literally just a couple of minutes whilst buying her grandson's dog Bruno a birthday bone.

When Elsie had come out of the pet shop with the bone her trolley was gone. She was really upset about it – the trolley was a great support to her as she wasn't that steady on her feet and tended to lean on the trolley to keep herself from falling over. She was telling the lady that she'd seen a man running down the road with it wearing a green t-shirt and shorts.

Sassie realised that this must have been the same man that broke into their house.

Sassie felt very angry and upset that not only did someone steal Charlie's laptop, but they also stole Elsie's trolley. Who could be that mean, she thought.

Poor Elsie, she loved Elsie, she was so kind, unlike some humans. She always had doggie treats in her trolley and she'd often stop and hand them out to Sassie and the gang.

Sassie kept herself to herself where humans were concerned. Other than her fabulous Charlie she wasn't that keen on them. But she had a soft spot for Elsie because although she looked frail and vulnerable, she was tough inside. Sassie admired that. Elsie was the same with humans as Sassie was with dogs, she wasn't that keen, she kept herself to herself.

They were quite similar really, Sassie thought.

Chapter 3
Jasper asks for help

Later that day, Sassie held an emergency meeting with the gang and told them all about the theft of Elsie's trolley. They all agreed that finding this thief was more important than any bone or ball. Even Magic agreed that rolling in stinky stuff would have to wait until after the thief was found.

To be honest, Magic thought to himself, I'm not sure that I feel like rolling in stinky stuff anyway. I think I'll just go and have a little nap while they come up with a plan.

The gang noticed Magic slope off for a nap. He did that a lot lately and sometimes he didn't even want to come out on 'Special Sundays'.

'Special Sundays' were when Mummy and Charlie didn't have work and the gang all got to go out in the red jeep. They'd go somewhere special like the beach, or the forest, or the lakes and just spend all day exploring. They were the best days and Magic used to love them, but recently he had sometimes been too tired to go. They all noticed it but no one wanted to say anything about it. They just hoped he'd get his Magic mojo back.

Jasper saw all this going on – Sassie being bossy, Magic nipping off for a nap, Rocco just looking handsome and perfect as always, staring intently at Sassie, and Flo looking a bit bewildered but ready to do whatever she was told.

You can all get on with it, Jasper thought to himself, but I'm going to be the star of the show for once. I'm going to catch that thief, having one eye is not going to hold me back, but I do need some help.

As much as he hated to admit it, having a young, strong dog with good eyesight like Rocco by his side would be sensible, so Jasper suggested that they should work together to find the thief.

Rocco loved the idea of working as a doggy detective with Jasper, his best friend. Not only would they be able to get Charlie her laptop back and Elsie her trolley back, he would also look like a hero in front of Sassie Snowdrops and his Mummy would think he was just the best dog that ever walked the cobbled streets of Chipping Dogbury.

"What we need to do, Rocco, is meet up in the middle of the night when everyone is asleep and we will patrol the High Street," said Jasper. "If the thief has stolen before he will steal again. Meet me in the garden tonight at midnight. Make sure you push the latch up on the window, but only very slightly so your Mummy doesn't notice and you can then slip out of the window when everyone is in bed."

"Got it," said Rocco in an excitable manner, "shall I wear a bandanna like a real doggy detective?"

"Really, Rocco," Jasper said in astonishment, "it's not about how you look. This is an important mission."

Rocco was a bit disappointed, as he thought he looked good in a bandanna and felt a bit empowered by it, like a superhero with his cape, but he didn't want to upset Jasper so he made a note not to put one on.

As they were making their plans, Sassie sashayed past and said, "Hello boys. What are you both up to?" Before they had chance to answer, she continued, "Well, whatever it is, it won't work out because you both always mess things up."

Jasper just glared at Sassie as best he could with one eye.

Rocco, as usual, just let out a contented sigh. He loved it when Sassie spoke to him – it didn't matter what she said, or how she said it, the fact she looked at him at all just made him feel amazing.

Chapter 4
The boys go on patrol

That evening, Rocco pretended to fall asleep as his Mummy kissed him goodnight and told him for the hundredth time about how he was rescued from a rubbish tip.

As soon as he heard his Mummy go upstairs Rocco opened his eyes. He listened out until he could hear her gentle snores, so he knew she was definitely asleep.

Rocco quickly and very quietly tip-pawed out of his basket and across the wooden floor, jumped up onto the windowsill and very delicately moved the window latch with his paw. He double-checked that his sister wasn't peeking, but she too was sleeping soundly.

Once outside on the High Street Rocco suddenly felt a little bit scared. He'd never been outside on his own before – well, not since his days on the streets in Romania – and he shuddered when he thought about those times. It was cold and very dark and he was just thinking about going back to his lovely warm basket when Jasper came out from behind the lamppost which he'd obviously just peed on.

"Hey, Rocco," said Jasper brightly. "Fair play, I thought you would be scared at the last minute and not come out."

Rocco was indignant. "What, me scared of the dark? I'm from Romania, all doggies in Romania are very brave," he said, with his fluffy white chest sticking out proudly. "I used to live on the streets you know."

Jasper didn't want to hear that story again so he quickly changed the subject. "Right, this is the plan, we are going to just stay low and in the shadows and walk around our High Street all night," he explained. "I chose this evening as there is a full moon and this will give us better light to see by. We know we are looking for a man who rides a bike with a basket on the front, wearing red shorts and a red t-shirt."

"I thought he was wearing green shorts and a green t-shirt?" Rocco piped up.

"No, definitely red," said Jasper, who was loving being in charge for once.

"Rocco, I will take this side of the High Street and you take the other. We are going to walk up and down and if we see the man we are looking for, bark like you've never barked before. Then I will run over and bark too until we wake the whole neighbourhood up so the thief will be caught and everyone will be very grateful to us and be so impressed by our courage."

Rocco was on it – up and down he walked, ready to bark, occasionally distracted by a cold chip or a bit of burger, which was a bonus. He could see Jasper doing the same, although he seemed to spend most of his time peeing on the lampposts.

After a couple of hours Rocco was getting bored and cold and if it wasn't for Jasper he'd have definitely sloped off home, but he couldn't leave his friend. So on and on the patrol went until the sun started breaking through the clouds and although the High Street looked really pretty, Rocco had had enough.

Just as he was about to cross the street to ask Jasper if he could go home, he suddenly heard his friend go into meltdown – he was barking like a wild thing.

Rocco ran as fast as his little legs could carry him to help Jasper, who had a man in red shorts and a red t-shirt pinned up against the wall, his bicycle lying on the floor. Rocco had to admit that, even with one eye, Jasper did look quite scary. Rocco joined in and before they knew it lights started to go on and windows were opened. Out came Mummy in her dressing gown looking far from pleased.

"What on earth is going on?" Mummy asked.

A small gathering had appeared on the street and all eyes were fixed on Jasper and Rocco… Jasper looked at Rocco and Rocco looked back at Jasper, his head bowed and his tail between his legs. Rocco couldn't understand why Mummy wasn't proud of their bravery like Jasper said she'd be.

"Why are you both barking at the Postman?" Mummy demanded. "In fact, why are you both outside on your own at this time of day?"

Rocco couldn't believe it, why did he ever listen to Jasper? They'd just woken everybody up and terrified the poor Postman. They'd be in big trouble now.

At that precise moment, Sassie came sashaying out of Charlie's house, she looked at them both as if they were completely ridiculous. "Are you two colour blind or just plain stupid?" she asked.

Rocco started explaining that he'd tried to tell Jasper that the thief had green shorts on, not red, but Sassie wasn't interested and she just walked off as he was mid-sentence. Her beautiful white-tipped tail gently knocked him in the face as she sashayed back into her house with Charlie, who asked her, "Sassie, why is it always those two that are so naughty, why can't they be more like you?"

Chapter 5

Goodbye, old friend

A few days after their midnight adventures, Rocco and Jasper were in the garden playing ball when they noticed Magic was just lying by the back fence.

"Jasper," Rocco said, "do you think Magic is alright? He has hardly moved today and when I took him the ball he didn't even look up."

"I don't know Rocco, but I must admit I'm a bit worried about him," Jasper said. "I think I'll go and get Charlie."

A short time later Jasper returned with Charlie, who immediately picked Magic up. The next thing they knew the front door banged shut and Charlie and Magic were gone.

Rocco had a funny feeling in his tummy, he didn't feel like playing ball anymore. He decided to go back to his house and seeing Flo on the sofa he jumped up and laid down next to her. Flo wasn't a cuddler, but she seemed to sense his unease and she moved closer to him so he could rest his head on her back.

In town, Charlie gently lifted Magic out of the car and carried him into the Vets. They both sat patiently waiting their turn and as they did so Charlie glanced around the waiting room.

Charlie couldn't believe her eyes – there was a scruffy-looking man sat opposite her and next to him was a shopping trolley that looked exactly like Elsie's. Inside the trolley something appeared to be moving.

"Excuse me, where did you get that trolley?" Charlie asked the man. He didn't answer, instead he just lowered his head and looked at the floor. "It's just that it looks very much like my friend Elsie's trolley, which was stolen last week," continued Charlie, refusing to be put off. But before the man could respond, Magic's name was called and Charlie had to gather him up and take him in to see the Vet.

The Vet looked at Charlie and then looked at Magic, then back to Charlie. The Vet looked sad and said to Magic, "Hello old boy, you're struggling a little there, come sit with me and let me check you over."

The Vet asked how old Magic was. "He's 15," Charlie said anxiously.

"Well," the Vet said gently, "in human years that's very old, it's difficult to say exactly, people often say every dog year equals seven human years, which would make him 105 in human terms. There's no exact science to it, but he is an old man and he's tired. He's telling you by not eating and not moving that he's had enough and he's ready to go. I'm really sorry, but there is nothing I can do."

Charlie knew what the Vet was saying was true and although she was still very sad to have to let Magic go, she knew it was the best and kindest thing to do. She had to be brave. She reminded herself that Magic had had the best, most amazing life.

Chapter 6
A chance encounter

Charlie couldn't see for tears as she left the Vets alone and headed out to the car park. She sat on a nearby bench and cried so hard she thought her heart would explode. Someone kindly walked over and handed her a tissue. Through her tears she looked up to say thank you and there stood in front of her was the man who she was sure had stolen Elsie's trolley.

"I am so sorry that you had to say goodbye to your beautiful dog today," he said, "and I am sorry, you're right, this is Elsie's trolley and I am the man who stole it. However, before I hand myself over to the Police let me please explain, because I am not really a bad person."

"My name is Jack," he continued, "and inside this trolley is my dog Polo." Charlie peered into the trolley and there before her was a fidgety-looking bundle of fluff that looked like a Poodle crossed with something, but she wasn't sure what.

Charlie had stopped crying and was focusing her attention on Jack, who was trying to explain himself. "I have become homeless because I don't have a job and I have no money," he said. "Polo suffers from epilepsy and she needs ongoing medication and that costs money that I just can't afford."

Then Jack bowed his head in shame and said guiltily, "Elsie's trolley isn't the only thing I stole, I also stole someone's laptop. I was knocking on doors looking for odd jobs I could do that could earn me enough money to pay for Polo's treatment.

No one was home at this one particular house and through the window I could see a laptop, so I smashed the window and stole the laptop. I was hoping to sell it for some money."

Charlie didn't tell Jack the laptop belonged to her as she wanted to hear what he'd done with it.

"I couldn't sell it though, I was too afraid I'd get caught," Jack continued. "I was going to return it but then Polo had another fit, so I came here instead."

"So," said Charlie, "if you didn't sell the laptop how were you going to pay for Polo's treatment today?"

"I had decided to leave Polo with the Vet to see if they could find her a better home," Jack said sorrowfully. "I love Polo so much and she is my world, but without a home or a job I can't look after her properly, I just can't afford her treatment. I know the Vet will find her a good home with someone who can give Polo all the things I can't."

"Jack, you may not have a home or a job or money but let's think about what you do have," said Charlie. "You have time and you have lots of love to give Polo and you seem like you want to do the right thing. You just don't know how to pay for Polo's medication."

"Let me think about this," said Charlie, pausing for a few minutes.

"I know," she said brightly, "let's go and see my friend Rachel and her dogs Rocco and Flo, they always come up with great ideas. Bring Polo with you and we'll all put our heads together."

Chapter 7
Jack makes amends

At Mummy's house later that day Charlie explained what Jack had done and why. Over tea and biscuits and doggy treats all round, Mummy came up trumps as Charlie expected.

"What we need to do is hold a charity concert in aid of Polo's medication!" Mummy announced. "We can ask Rocco's band to play and we can close off the street. We can ask the Butchers to serve hot dogs and veggie burgers and we can ask Brook to make Dogtails. It will be so much fun and, hopefully, we will raise lots of money for Polo and maybe for some other doggies too."

"What a great idea," said Charlie, "let's do it! Come on Jack, we've got things to do, people to see, we're gonna make this happen."

"Hang on a minute," said Mummy, holding up her hand, "before you start dashing around – Jack, you have to go and take Elsie's trolley back."

"Oh yes, and I would like my laptop back please!" Charlie piped up.

Jack couldn't believe it – he really liked Charlie and here she was trying to help him even though it was her laptop he'd stolen. He felt awful.

Charlie sensed how bad Jack was feeling and, turning to him, said, "Jack, everyone makes mistakes and I know you were only trying to find a way to help Polo. You are a kind person and I know it's hard to ask for help. However, sometimes the hardest thing to do takes courage. Come on, I'll come with you to see Elsie."

And off they both went to make amends and start making plans for the doggy charity day.

Chapter 8
The doggy charity day

A few weeks later, on a lovely sunny day, the High Street was buzzing. There were people putting up rides, men closing off the street to traffic, candy floss machines were being set up and at the far end a big stage was being put up in readiness for the band.

Rocco couldn't wait to get out on the High Street and see what was going on. Flo, as always, went straight to the Butchers so Rocco went down to see his friends in the band.

Sassie, Charlie and Jasper were wandering up and down spreading the word that there was a little doggy needing some support and trying to get people to donate to the doggy aid fund. Jasper had finally found his calling – people were loving him and his one eye and donations were piling in.

Mummy was trying to keep tabs on Rocco but she was also asking around to see if anyone could offer Jack a job, as she knew that the money raised by the charity day wouldn't support Polo's medication forever. She'd had some lovely conversations and there seemed to be a lot of goodwill, but no one had any work.

Mummy smiled as she saw Rocco with the band, he was loving the attention. The band had bought him a new bandanna with their name on it and he had that on and was high-fiving so much that she thought he might topple off the stage.

She walked over to Rocco and started talking to the lead singer, Ed. As they were chatting she mentioned that she really wanted to find Jack some work so that once the money raised ran out he would be able to support himself and Polo on his own.

"Well, funnily enough," Ed said, "our Roadie has just left us, so we could do with another pair of hands. Tell Jack to come over and we'll have a chat. No promises though – he'd have to work hard!"

"Oh, that's amazing Ed, I totally understand that Jack will have to prove himself to you. I'll go and get him now," said Mummy excitedly, grabbing Rocco's lead and dashing off to find Jack.

A few hours later, when what had been a fabulous doggy charity day was starting to draw to a close, Mummy looked over and could see Jack helping the band load their instruments into their van. She smiled to herself, hoping Jack would pass the test. He certainly looked like he fitted in – there was lots of chat and laughter and Polo was snuggled in the back of the band's van on a lovely blanket being cuddled by one of the backing singers.

"I do believe, darling Rocco, we have found Jack a job. Let's hope he works hard and keeps it," said Mummy, looking down lovingly at her handsome little man. Rocco looked up at his Mummy, she really was the kindest Mummy in the world. He'd had an awesome day.

Rocco had quite liked the idea of being a Roadie himself, but then he realised he'd really miss his Mummy and Sassie and Charlie and Jasper and even Flo Bear Star. He was a Rock Star at heart he decided, but in reality he didn't want to go anywhere other than his lovely cottage in Chipping Dogbury.

"Of course, I could have joined the band and travelled all over the country," Rocco said to Sassie as they all walked home together.

"Sure you could have Rocco," smiled Sassie. "You'd better go home now – I think your Mummy has a nice milky water waiting for you."

"Oh, does she? Bye Sassie, I'll see you tomorrow," Rocco yelped, and with that he ran in through his gate and was gone.

After his milky water Rocco snuggled down exhausted in his basket and his Mummy did what she did every night at bedtime.

She put a lovely soft blanket over him and started telling him the story of how he had been found on a rubbish tip in Romania, tired and hungry on a freezing cold night and how he had been so brave travelling on a bus all the way to England and… he was gone, snoring softly.

Mummy stood up, went over to Flo, who was already asleep, and put a lovely soft blanket over her too, then put the night light on and went up to bed.

What a great day, she thought, we should make the charity doggy day an annual event. I'll have to speak to Charlie about that tomorrow…

Courage is at the heart of this book.

Sometimes in life we can feel scared or anxious like Jack. These feelings can make us feel sad and worried. You might get "butterflies in your stomach" when you have to do something, or say something – for example if you have to speak in front of your class, or if you have a new activity club to join. These feelings are perfectly normal and often when you tell someone what you are worried about it can become less scary.

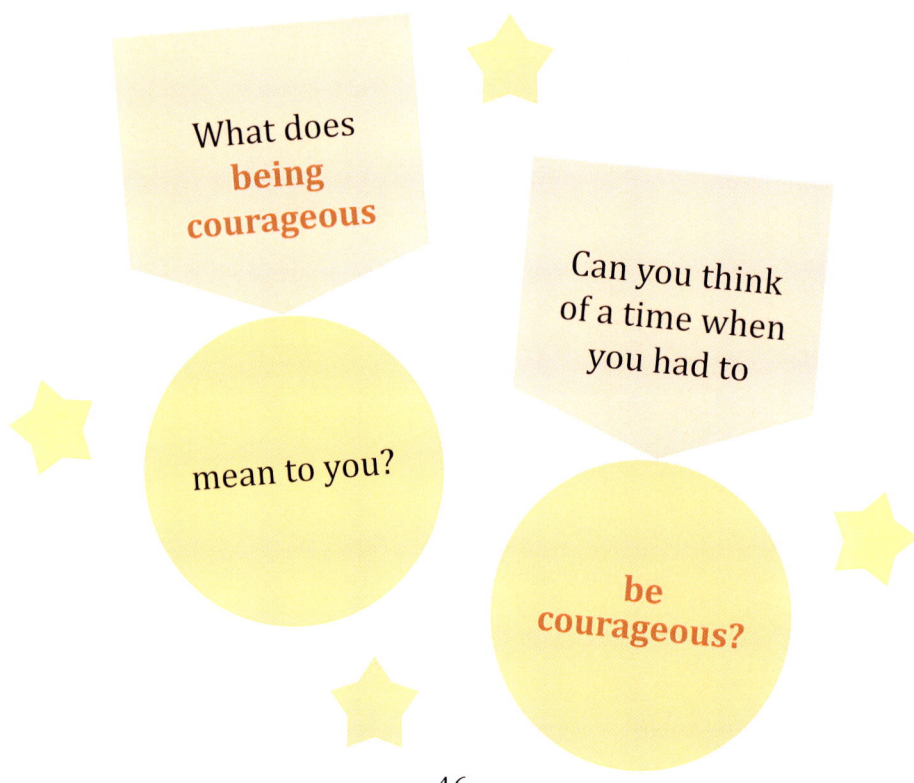

What does being courageous mean to you?

Can you think of a time when you had to be courageous?